Huxley Pig the Clown

Rodney Peppé

WARNE

For Biddy Floyer

Another book about Huxley Pig
Here Comes Huxley Pig

FREDERICK WARNE

Published by the Penguin Group
27 Wrights Lane, London W8 5TZ, England
Viking Penguin Inc., 40 West 23rd Street, New York, New York 10010, USA
Penguin Books Australia Ltd, Ringwood, Victoria, Australia
Penguin Books Canada Ltd, 2801 John Street, Markham, Ontario, Canada L3R 1B4
Penguin Books (NZ) Ltd, 182-190 Wairau Road, Auckland 10, New Zealand

Penguin Books Ltd, Registered Offices: Harmondsworth, Middlesex, England

First published 1989
10 9 8 7 6 5 4 3 2 1

British Library Cataloguing in Publication Data available

ISBN 0 7232 3621 6

Printed and bound in Great Britain by William Clowes Ltd,
Beccles and London

Huxley Pig was rummaging
through his clothes.

"Today," said Huxley,
"I think I'll be a clown
and practise some tricks."

First he tried to
stand on a ball.

Sitting might
be easier.

Next he stood
on his head.

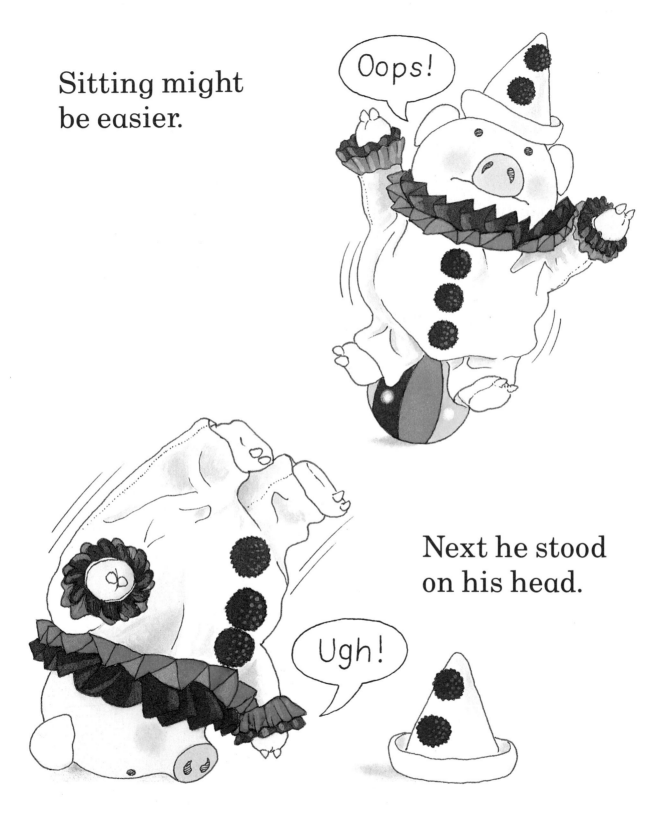

Now for some juggling...

He tried jumping through a hoop.

Huxley was
sure he
could walk
the tightrope.

My best
trick!

But the rope broke,
because Huxley
was much too heavy!

A gust of wind
from the window
lifted the quilt
on his bed.

"It's just like
a circus tent,"
thought Huxley.
And he went
inside . . .

He met the ringmaster of the circus.
"You're late!" said the ringmaster, waving a
programme with Huxley's picture on it.
"Horace will help you."

"Don't worry," said Horace, rather loudly.
"I'll catch you when you – I mean, *if* you fall."

Huxley performed his tricks perfectly,
helped by Horace . . .

and not
helped by
Horace!

He balanced upside-down on a tightrope
and played a trumpet. The audience
laughed and cheered.

He chased Horace in his crazy car.
They laughed and cheered even louder.

Then on came the dancing girls.
And Huxley blushed, very pink.

Everyone laughed. Even the ringmaster.
And especially Horace!

In his confusion Huxley forgot
he was only a clown. "Now I'll do a triple
somersault," he announced.

"And I'll catch you," said Horace,
with a wicked grin.

Huxley started his somersault.
The audience held its breath.

"You were supposed to *catch* me, Horace!"
said Huxley as he fell . . .

. . . with a BUMP!
"Was I dreaming, or was I marvellous?"
wondered Huxley, as he poked out
his head from under the quilt.

Then he saw the circus programme,
with his picture on the cover.
"What a magic adventure!" thought Huxley.

Huxley was all tucked up for the night.
And then he suddenly remembered.
"That Horace pinched my hat!"

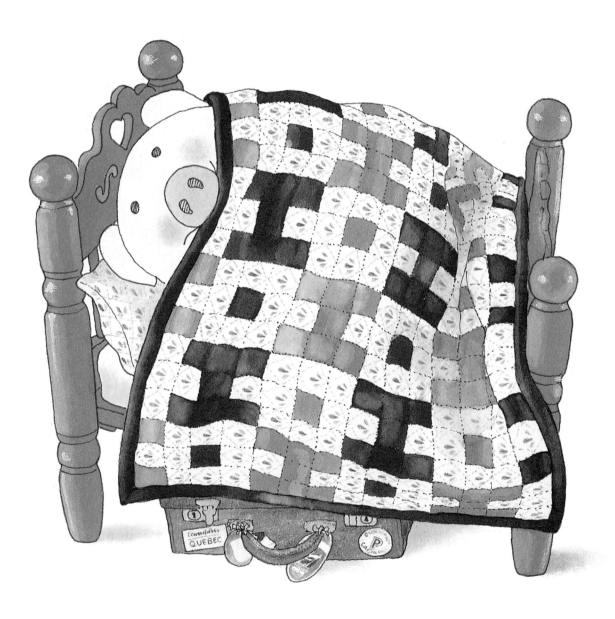